Kevin's
First Flight

Written by Noah Emery

Illustrations by Lindsay Coequit

D1232762

ISBN 978-1949248-104
Copyright©2020 Noah Emery
All Rights Reserved

No part of this publication may be reproduced in any material form (including photocopying or storing in any medium by electronic means and whether or not transiently or incidentally to some other use of this publication) without the written permission of the copyright holder except in accordance with the provisions of Title 17 of the United States Code.

Published for the author by:
Orange Frazer Press
37½ West Main St.
P.O. Box 214
Wilmington, OH 45177

For price and shipping information, call: 937.382.3196
Or visit: www.orangefrazer.com

Book and cover design by: Kelly Schutte and Orange Frazer Press

Library of Congress Control Number: 2019912626

Printed in China
10/01/2019
Batch #: 83798

First Printing

To my wife, Katie.
Your strength inspires me every single day.
And to my son, Gregory Jack.
Chase all your dreams and challenge the unknown.
~ Noah

To my husband, Seth.
These paintings were only made possible
through your endless love and support.
And to my daughter, Cora.
Stay sweet and strong. You will be able to accomplish
anything your heart desires.
~ Lindsay

Kevin the cardinal
starts stretching his wings.

He's getting ready
for what the day brings.

Kevin is a bird,
with bright red feathers.

Today he will try to fly,
so on a branch he tethers.

Kevin feels nervous,
but takes to the air.

He leaps toward the sky by moving
his wings,
ascending into the clouds without a scare.

Overcome with joy,
Kevin soars higher.

He sings in stride as time goes by,
imagining how his day will transpire.

Off in the distance,
Kevin sees flowers.

Turning the red quill of his wings down,
he finds where he will spend a few hours.

Touching down safely,
Kevin looks around.

Seeing black, green, and brown,
he eats the seeds on the ground.

The flowers are tall,
full of bright yellow.

Kevin preens at his red-feathered gown,
but jumps up, hearing a loud bellow.

Kevin hears thunder
and chirps back with fear.

When the sky turns dark and rain falls,
he worries as the storm clouds near.

The wind whips and snaps,
but he finds a limb.

As lightning strikes down from the squall,
Kevin's situation looks grim.

Not safe in the tree,
Kevin forms a plan.

He recalls a barn that's not too tall,
and has an awning along its span.

As the storm passes,
Kevin sits in awe.

An arch of color paints the dusk
    before night,
the rainbow is a wonder that has no flaw.

Kevin is flying,
with his wings stretched out wide.

He passes through the night's light,
using moon beams as his guide.

Kevin is a bird,
with a bright red crest.

Pleased with a successful first flight,
he is ready to return to his nest.

Kevin the cardinal rests his tired wings.

He's excited for what tomorrow brings.

Noah Emery

Noah was born and raised in Knoxville, Illinois. He graduated from Monmouth College in Monmouth, Illinois, where he majored in political science. In his professional life, Noah has worked in higher education, administering financial aid since 2011. *Kevin's First Flight* is his debut children's book. Noah and his wife, Katie, live in Hamilton, Ohio. They have a young son and two Golden Retrievers.

Lindsay Cocquit

Lindsay was born and raised in Burlington, Iowa. She attended Monmouth College in Monmouth, Illinois, where she graduated with a degree in art and education. She is currently a high school art teacher. She also works with Art at the Bodega, an art studio in Washington, Illinois. Lindsay and her family live in Peoria, Illinois.